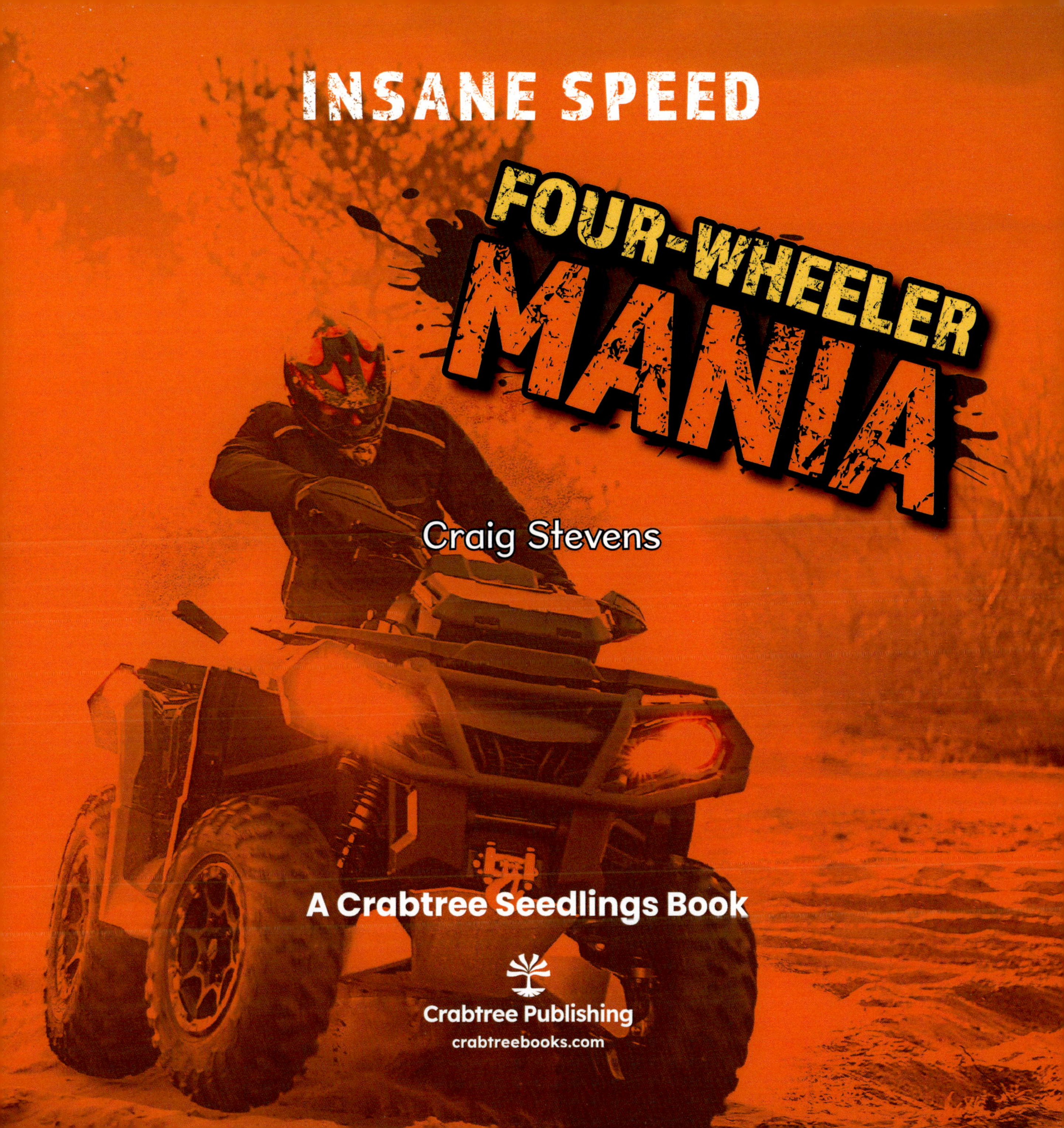

INSANE SPEED

FOUR-WHEELER MANIA

Craig Stevens

A Crabtree Seedlings Book

Crabtree Publishing
crabtreebooks.com

UTV
utility terrain vehicle
VS

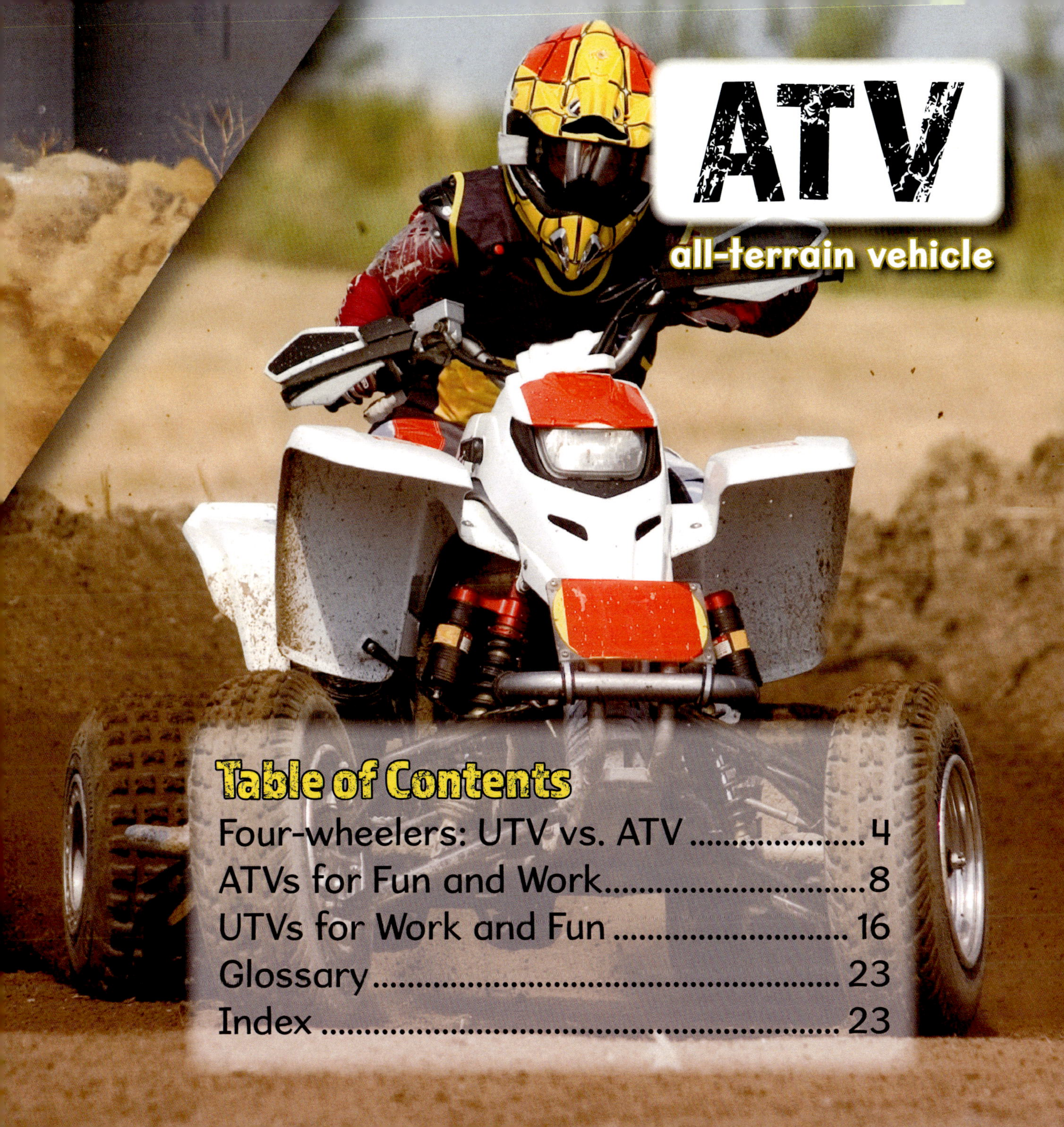

Table of Contents

Four-wheelers: UTV vs. ATV

UTVs and ATVs are four-wheelers. Four-wheelers are made for riding over rough **terrain**.

UTV (utility terrain vehicle)

Four-wheelers are also called quad bikes.

ATV (all-terrain vehicle)

UTVs and ATVs can drive through or over almost anything.

Four-wheelers have good balance when handled correctly.

ATVs for Fun and Work

The ATV was one of the first four-wheelers. It was built for **recreation**.

The first ATV was built in the early 1980s.

seat - made for two riders, plus storage rack
gas tank - holds up to 3 gallons (11.35 liters) of gas
muffler - reduces noise of exhaust being released
chain and sprocket - turns the wheel
ATV
engine - powerful enough to haul things attached to ATV

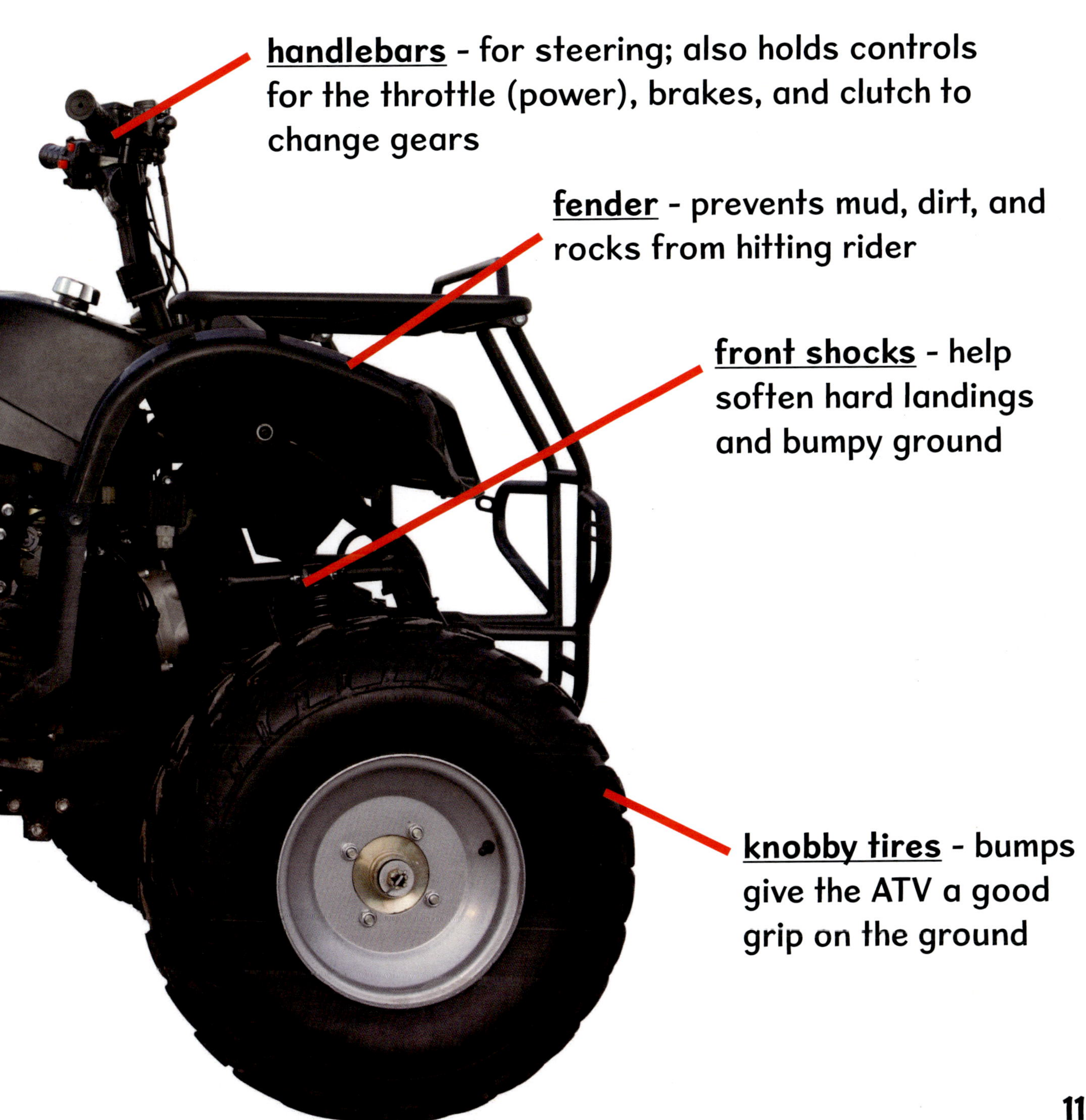

handlebars - for steering; also holds controls for the throttle (power), brakes, and clutch to change gears

fender - prevents mud, dirt, and rocks from hitting rider

front shocks - help soften hard landings and bumpy ground

knobby tires - bumps give the ATV a good grip on the ground

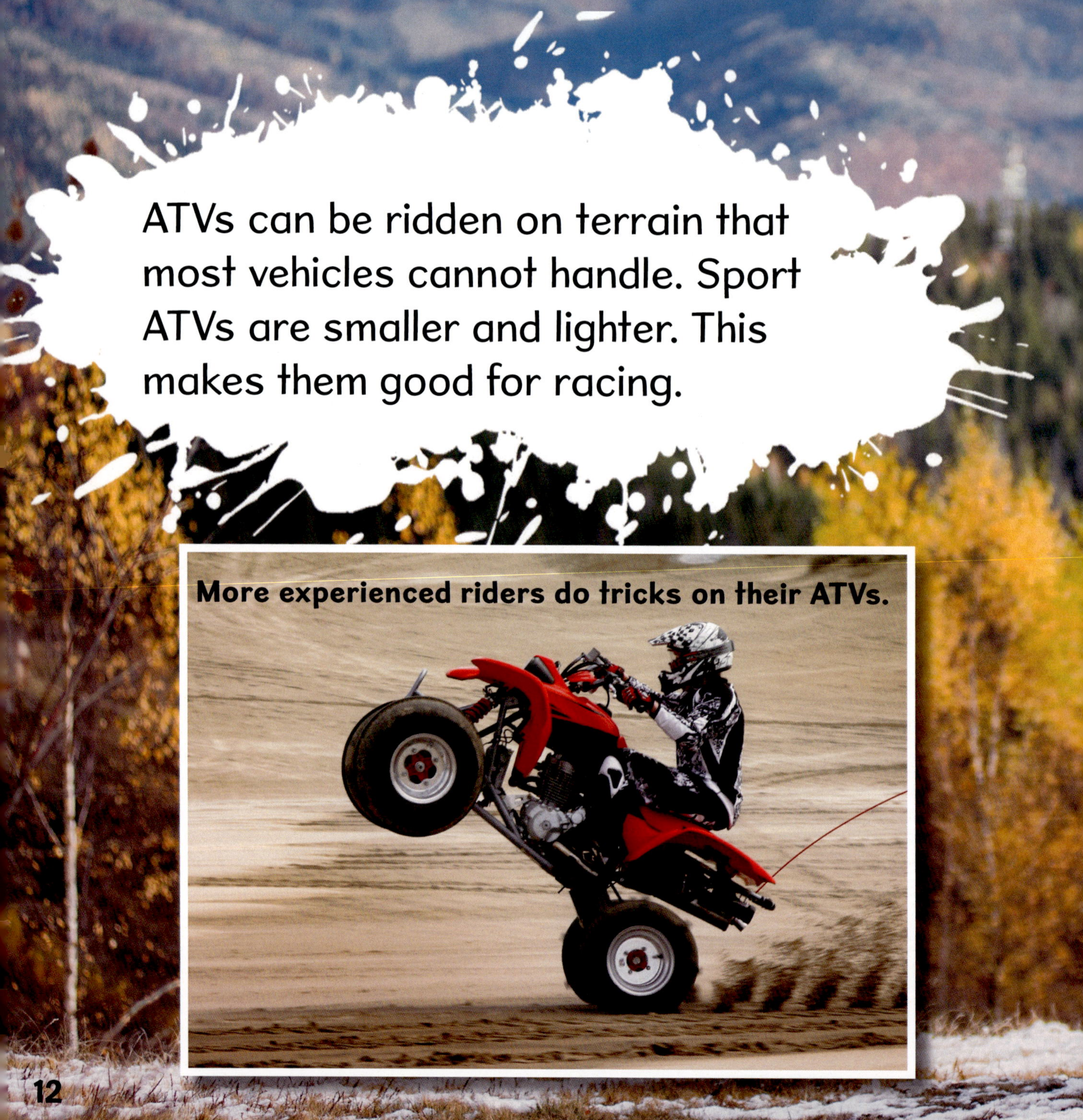

ATVs can be ridden on terrain that most vehicles cannot handle. Sport ATVs are smaller and lighter. This makes them good for racing.

More experienced riders do tricks on their ATVs.

Some four-wheelers can carry two people.

Many farmers use ATVs for work. ATVs have good pulling power.

CHECK OIL
DAILY

UTVs for Work and Fun

After the ATV, a new off-road design became popular—the UTV. The UTV is smaller but **stable**.

Some UTVs have a rear cargo hold, or bed, like a pick-up truck.

Two people can ride side by side in a UTV.

UTVs became popular for their looks and speed. The fast speeds made them perfect for racing too.

door straps - mesh and nylon straps to keep rider safe

seats - two bucket seats plus safety belts

driving and taillights - allow for safe, nighttime driving

muffler - reduces noise of exhaust being released

Suspension - helps keep the UTV stable on bumpy ground

steering wheel - used with pedals (not shown) to drive the UTV
roll bar - protects riders in case the UTV rolls over
body - made from light material with **decals** added
knobby tires - bumps give the UTV a good grip on the ground
front brakes - used to stop the UTV
UTV

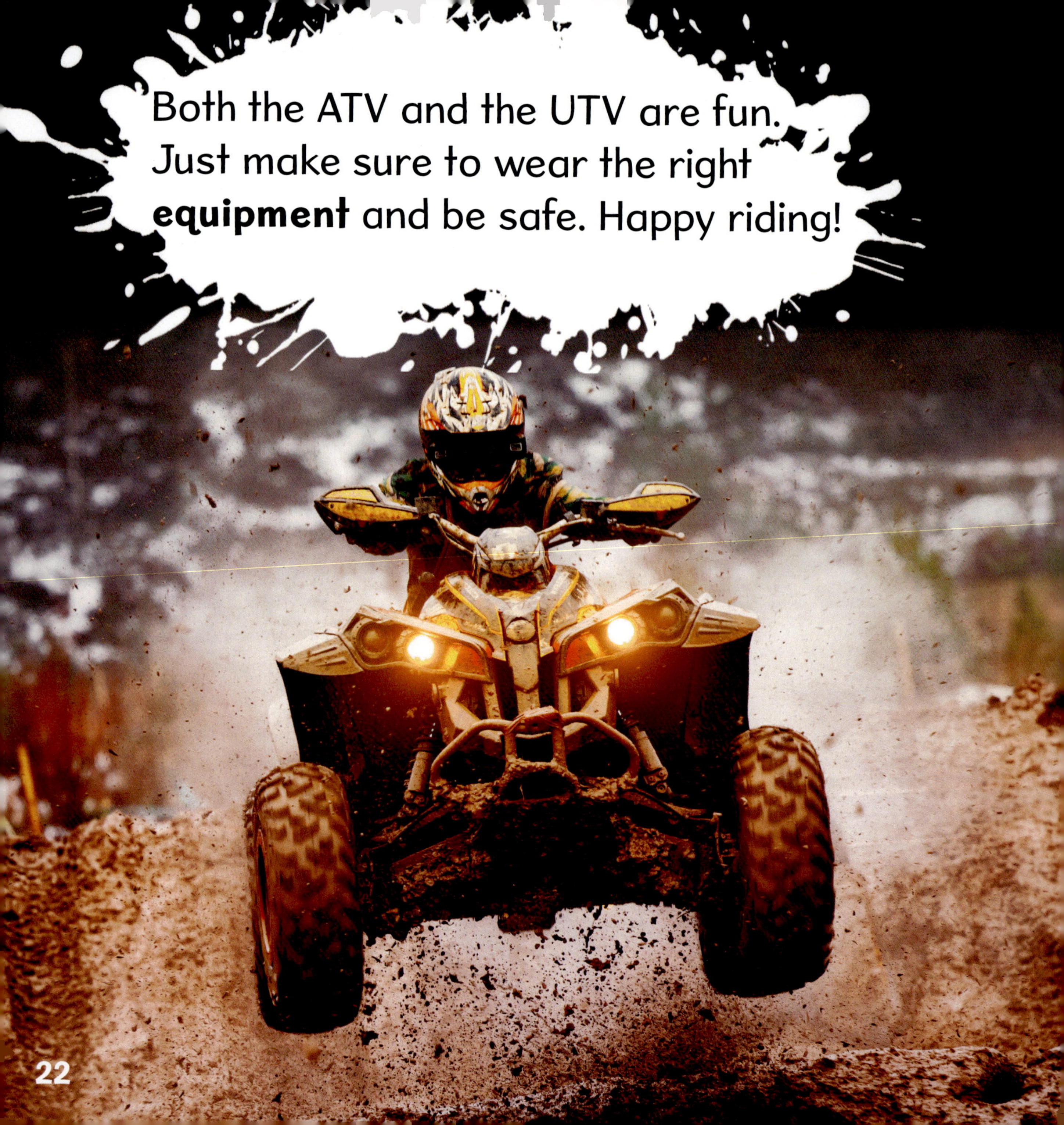

Both the ATV and the UTV are fun. Just make sure to wear the right **equipment** and be safe. Happy riding!

Glossary

decals (DEE-kalz): Stickers—sometimes very large—showing cool designs

equipment (uh-KWIP-muhnt): Clothing or tools that makes an activity safer, easier, or more comfortable; *a helmet is equipment that makes riding a four-wheeler safer.*

recreation (rek-ree-AY-shuhn): Hobbies and sports that people like to do in their spare time

stable (STAY-buhl): Firm and steady

terrain (tuh-RAYN): Any kind of ground, such as rocky, sandy, or muddy

Index

School-to-Home Support for Caregivers and Teachers

This book helps children grow by letting them practice reading. Here are a few guiding questions to help the reader build his or her comprehension skills. Possible answers appear here in red.

Before Reading

- **What do I think this book is about?** I think this book is about riding in a four-wheeler. I think this book is about four-wheeler races.
- **What do I want to learn about this topic?** I want to learn more about all-terrain vehicles. I want to learn where I can find an ATV course to ride on.

During Reading

- **I wonder why...** I wonder why farmers use a UTV instead of a tractor. I wonder why someone invented the ATV.
- **What have I learned so far?** I have learned that four-wheelers are made for riding over rough terrain. I have learned that there are races for four-wheelers.

After Reading

- **What details did I learn about this topic?** I have learned that many farmers use ATVs for work because they have good pulling power. I have learned that knobby tires give ATVs a good grip on the ground so they don't get stuck.
- **Read the book again and look for the glossary words.** I see the word *terrain* on page 4 and the word *stable* on page 16 . The other glossary words are found on page 23.

Crabtree Publishing

crabtreebooks.com 800-387-7650

Hardcover 978-1-0396-4484-7
Paperback 978-1-0396-4675-9

Printed in Canada
042024/CP20240422

Published in Canada
Crabtree Publishing
616 Welland Avenue
St. Catharines, Ontario
L2M 5V6

Published in the United States
Crabtree Publishing
347 Fifth Avenue
Suite 1402-145
New York, NY 10016

Written by: Craig Stevens
Print book version produced jointly with Blue Door Education in 2023

Photo Credits: Cover © Artur Didyk/Shutterstock.com; title page and pages 4-5 (in background), pages 6-7 (background photo): © 6okean | istockphoto; page 2: © Snap2Art_RF | istockphoto; page 3: © 450yamaha | istockphoto; page 4: inset photo © pixinoo | istockphoto; page 6: inset photo © Gunter Nuyts/Shutterstock.com; pages 8-9: background photo © FS-Stock | istockphoto, inset photo; page 8: © Rainmaker47 https://creativecommons.org/licenses/by-sa/3.0/deed.en; pages 10-11: © kamski | istockphoto; pages 12-13: background photo © anatoliy_gleb | istockphoto; page 12: inset photo © shutterbugger | istockphoto; pages 14-15: background photo © Pomemick | istockphoto; page 14: inset photo © Kosorukov Dmitry/Shutterstock.com; pages 16-17: background photo © Page Light Studios | istockphoto; page 16: inset photo © Tommy Liggett/Shutterstock.com; pages 18-19: background photo © OgnjenO/Shutterstock.com; page 18: inset photo © Snap2Art_RF | istockphoto; pages 20-21: © valio84sl | istockphoto; page 22: © HeyPhoto/Shutterstock.com; page 23: © Toa55/Shutterstock.com

Library and Archives Canada Cataloguing in Publication
Available at the Library and Archives Canada

Library of Congress Cataloging-in-Publication Data
Available at the Library of Congress